The Adventures of The Thundering Whales

Thunder

Sapphire

Flukie

The Dreaded Weaved Catcher

Author
Marine Life Sculptor
Stephen Vadakin

Check out Stephen's web-site

www.thunderingwhales.com

Where you can accompany Stephen on a whale watch off the coast of Cape Cod that he filmed himself. See all of his marine life sculptures and learn all kinds of great things about marine life.

Quick. Raise your hand if you knew that a dolphin was a whale. Not a lot of hands up, are there? Not even mine. I was pleasantly surprised at how much I learned while reading The Adventures of the Thundering Whales. I remember wishing I had a child to read the book to. Then I realized what I really wanted was a movie version of the book, with all its characters portrayed in glorious color, like a "Finding Nemo", but with so much more to say.

Most of the time I find Children's books that anthropomorphize their animal characters lose their ability to teach. An animal (or mammal, or fish, or bird, etc.) cannot take on human attributes without losing some of their own. But the author, Stephen Vadakin, has spent enough time studying marine life to allow his characters to keep their real life tendencies and reactions as true as possible. For instance, did you know that sperm whale and squid were enemies?

Vadakin not only tells a great tale, with danger and excitement and fully fleshed out characters; he includes a vocabulary lesson at the end of each chapter so that everyone involved knows what plankton, krill, fluke and bioluminescence are.

The lessons of friendship, helping and putting aside ones differences for the greater good are all demonstrated in the tale. The one thing that I found awkward was the use of third person, present tense throughout the story. It took a while to get used to hearing a children's story in present tense. I also would have enjoyed many more graphics. I suppose this is why I'd like to see this made into a movie. The different characters, while mostly in the whale family, are so distinct that only animation could do it justice.

*We Would love to see this Children's book
made into an animated movie.*

CHAPTER 1
The Gold Medallion

Out in the ocean off the coast of the Emerald Isle, three young dolphins* are playing. Their names are Thunder, Flukie, and Sapphire. Their mothers, fathers, and all their other family members are swimming nearby, too.

Thunder's father is the school master. He often uses his deep, strong voice to tell the children stories and legends about the past. Today, he uses his voice to call out to the young dolphins.

"Don't swim too far away!" Thunder's father calls out. "And always remember to be careful of the danger above the waves!"

Thunder, Flukie, and Sapphire know the sound of danger. It is a humming sound above the waves. The humming sound comes from a fishing boat that drags a net in the water.

While the three young dolphins enjoy their fun and games, the swordfish patrol is swimming by. This type of fish has a long, thin pointed nose that looks like a sword. The 20 swordfish swim through the area to help any creature who is in danger. Their job is to protect all creatures.

The swordfish patrol members are similar to police officers, but they are a strange bunch. For one thing, some of their outfits are too big and some are too small. Many buttons are missing from their uniforms. Their uniforms don't match.

But they take their job seriously.

As they swim by, they stop to speak to the dolphins.

"Is everything OK here?" asks the leader of the swordfish patrol, Captain Siringgo.

"Yes, everything is great! Thank you officer," Thunder, Sapphire, and Flukie reply.

Today Thunder, Flukie, and Sapphire are enjoying a beautiful day. The water is blue-green and the sun is bright yellow. The dolphins race, breach,* and jump high out of the water.

"Hey! Watch me jump out of the water," Thunder yells to his friends.

He hurls himself into the air and does a flip, then a perfect dive back into the water.

Thunder loves to show off.

Sapphire says, "Oh, yeah? Well, watch ME!"

She jumps out of the water and gets almost as high as Thunder had breached. She does a double flip. Around and around she goes, and back into the water.

Flukie rockets out of the water with his big flukes higher than the others. He does one flip and he tries to do another, but can't make it and falls back down into the water with a belly-flop, splashing water all over his friends. They all laugh.

The three dolphins love to see all the different creatures under the water and above the waves. They love all the different things in their ocean world.

Thunder is the biggest of the young dolphins. He was named after his grandfather who was the leader of their pod *. Thunder is big and strong, just like his grandfather. Grandpa Thunder once saved his family from the Giant Weaved Catcher.

Human people have a different name for the Giant Weaved Catcher. They call it a fishing net. This net is part of a boat called a fishing trawler*. The fishing trawler makes a humming sound above the waves.

Grandpa Thunder's family was trapped in the fishing net. There was a storm in the ocean. The waves were very big. The fishing trawler was in trouble, and was sinking into the water. The dolphins and all the other fish were in great danger. Grandpa Thunder found a way to cut the fishing net, and pulled the family out of danger. The dolphins looked back and saw the fishing trawler and Giant Weaved Catcher fall down, down, down, to the very bottom of the ocean.

Grandpa Thunder was such a hero that the captain of the swordfish patrol gave him a medal of honor.

In the shallow areas of the ocean, the dolphins can swim at the very bottom. There are lots of things for them to look at and play with down there. They love to swim around big, old ships that sank a long time ago. The bottom of the ocean is covered with hundreds of shipwrecks.

One day, Thunder found a special gold medallion*. He found it in a sunken Pirate ship. The dolphins were swimming near this sunken Pirate ship when Thunder saw a shiny flash through one of the ship's windows.

Thunder called out to his friends, "Come with me! I saw something."

Flukie, Sapphire, and Thunder approached the old tall-masted shipwreck. It looked very scary. There was rotten wood everywhere.

"Let's go inside the ship," Thunder said.

Flukie said, "Let's go this way. I see something shiny."

They swam to the back of the ship. Humans would call this part of the ship the Captain's Quarters. To the dolphins, this room inside of the ship was very mysterious and a little spooky. The door to the room was hanging off one hinge, swaying back and forth slowly. They swam into the room and explored many strange things. There was an old carved wooden table. Little minnows* swam in and out of a bookshelf filled with holes. The books had rotted away a long time ago. A rusted pitcher on the floor was covered with seaweed. An old metal chest sat in a corner, rusted and empty.

Then they saw it: a skeleton! It was the skeleton of a man, sitting in the captain's chair. There were big, black holes where its eyes used to be. The skeleton wore a pirate's outfit. He had been sitting down there for a long time.

At first, the dolphins were a little scared of the skeleton. But skeletons are just old bones. They can't hurt anyone. So Sapphire, Thunder and Flukie swam closer to the skeleton and saw a necklace around its neck. The necklace had a big, shiny gold medallion hanging from it. Dolphins love bright, shiny things.

Flukie said, "It is a beautiful necklace. Can we have it?"

Sapphire laughed and said, "Yes. I think that the skeleton is not using it anymore!"

4

Sapphire took the big gold medallion in her mouth and pulled. The cord around the pirate's neck flashed for a second and dissolved. Then it was gone. At the same time, the gold medallion flashed brightly.

The dolphins looked at each other. They were amazed when the gold medallion flashed like that. It flashed as bright as the sun.

Sapphire said, "Thunder saw the necklace first, so he should have it." They all agreed.

Sapphire made a cord for the necklace. She took a piece of seaweed she found floating in the water. She put the seaweed string through the hole in the gold medallion. Then she put it around Thunder's neck.

They all laughed and made up a new song. It was called "Thunder: King of the Sea." And the song goes:

Thunder, Thunder, king of the sea
Thunder, Thunder, best friend to you and me.

- **Did you know that dolphins are whales? Dolphins are one of the smallest members of the whale family.**
- **Breach: A leap out of the water by a dolphin or whales**
- **Fishing Trawler: A boat used to catch fish with a net.**
- **Pod: A group of dolphins or whales.**
- **Medallion: A large old coin.**
- **Minnows: A type of small, silver-colored fish.**

CHAPTER 2
The Weaved Catcher

Sapphire is a bit of a tomboy. She swims very fast and breaches out of the water almost as high as the boys, as we know. She has sparkling eyes and a pretty blue swirl on her skin. She also seems to have a bit of a crush on Thunder.

Flukie is the fastest swimmer. He got his name because he has bigger flukes* than his friends. He is also missing a piece of his dorsal fin.* Dolphins who have bigger flukes are faster swimmers. Flukie wins almost every race.

The dolphins have been warned about a giant weaved catcher that swims through the ocean. This beast catches many dolphins. When the giant weaved catcher traps the dolphins, their friends and family never see them again.

Humans call the weaved catcher a net. This net is attached to a fishing boat called a trawler. The young dolphins don't know these human words, but they do know about the humming sound. They know that when they hear the humming sound, the weaved catcher is near. They know they must swim away from the humming sound as fast as they can.

The giant weaved catcher is very near. Thunder, Sapphire, and Flukie are in great danger. But right now they are playing and they don't hear the humming sound.

Suddenly the danger is upon them! In one swoop, Thunder is caught in the net. Luckily, this net is not attached to the trawler anymore. Yet Thunder is trapped in the net, and his life is in great danger. He is so scared, he struggles and flips around. This causes him to be trapped even tighter in the net. He can't even move.

Unable to swim, he starts falling. Thunder falls down farther and farther into the deep ocean. "Help! Help me!" he cries.

Sapphire and Flukie don't waste even one second. They swim down, down, to where Thunder is caught, helpless in the net. They try to free him from the net. Sapphire looks into Thunder's eyes and they both start to cry.

Flukie and Sapphire can't swim any deeper to save Thunder. They can only watch their friend fall.

As he falls, Thunder sees the edge of the ocean shelf and the coral reef pass him. One hundred feet, 200 feet, 300 feet ... down and down he goes.

Sapphire and Flukie run out of breath. They must swim back up to the surface of the ocean to get more air. They are heartbroken. They know Thunder can't get any air.

But a strange thing is happening to Thunder. As he falls farther and farther down, far away from his friends, his golden medallion suddenly flashes with light. Thunder sees that he is inside a giant clear bubble. Both he and the net are inside this bubble.

Thunder has fallen hundreds and hundreds of feet down to the deepest depths of the great ocean. He has fallen deeper than any bottlenose dolphin has ever gone before, and stayed alive.

"I must be inside a magic bubble or I would be dead," Thunder says to himself. "I can breathe! What is this bubble about? Why did my medallion shine so brightly?"

He looks around and sees all kinds of strange-looking creatures that he has never seen before. They all stare back as if they have never seen anyone like *him* before, either. In that instant, everything around him begins to shake and rock. All the strange-looking creatures take off as if they are swimming for their lives. It's an underwater earthquake! Thunder is pushed hard against the ocean's rocky walls. Huge rocks fall all around him. Still inside the bubble, Thunder sees a cave entrance. Suddenly, he is being sucked into an underwater cave. He looks behind him and sees giant rocks covering the entrance to the cave.

Inside the underwater cave, Thunder is sucked upward through a passageway. He is moving quite fast. He is confused and dazed. Suddenly, he pops up to the top of the passageway. Now he is floating in a river. It is a river inside of a cave.

Thunder is inside of a net, and the net is inside of a bubble. The bubble is in a river, and the river is in a cave, and the cave is deep down in the ocean!

Whew! That is sure a lot to think about, but Thunder has no time to think right now.

Suddenly, the bubble pops. Thunder is startled by the loud pop. He breaches from the bubble, dives into the water, and floats to the surface of the river. He has escaped from the net.

Thunder shakes his head. He cannot believe what just happened to him. Slowly looking around, he sees that the cave is gigantic. The river is very long and there is a glow all around him. It is a magical glow and it lights up the cave. He looks closer and sees thousands of tiny fireflies. They are all looking at him, wondering who and what he is. There is air in the cave, so he can breathe air when he wants to. He is out of danger for a little while.

But Thunder is worried. "How am I going to get out of here?" he wonders.

Looking far, far down the river, he sees a glimmer of light. The light must be more than a mile away. Does the light mean there is a way out of this cave? Thunder has no idea.

"How will Flukie and Sapphire know I'm not dead? How can I tell my Mom and Dad I'm OK but I need help?"

Thunder gets an answer to his questions right away when he sees something floating on the surface of the river. It is an old bottle with a big cork plugged in the top. He has an idea. He grabs the bottle, takes the medallion from his neck and puts it in the bottle. He decides to swim back to the entrance of the cave to see if he can find a way to get the bottle out into the ocean. If he can put the bottle back into the ocean, maybe Flukie and Sapphire will find it and rescue him from this cave.

Thunder begins to feel weak and dizzy as he swims back down the passage from the cave to the ocean. He feels the pressure of the ocean depths squeeze against his body. It feels very tight against his skin and bones, and it hurts him. It takes him a long, long time to reach the cave entrance.

Finally, he reaches the entrance. Giant rocks are blocking the cave entrance. He can't get out.

Small fish are swimming through the cracks between the giant rocks. The bottle will fit. He pushes the bottle through. He turns and heads back to the cave.

It takes him a long time to get back to the river in the cave. Once there, Thunder feels dizzy and very, very tired. He takes a deep breath. He decides he will take a nap now.

- **Fluke: A dolphin's tail is split at the end. These two halves of a dolphin's tail are called flukes.**
- **Dorsal Fin: The fin at the top of a dolphin's back.**

CHAPTER 3
Old Blue One

Way up at the surface of the ocean, Sapphire and Flukie had heard Thunder's distress calls. They felt terrible they could not rescue him. Then they heard the rumbling earthquake, and they became even more worried about their friend.

A bottle suddenly pops up to the surface. Sapphire swims over and grabs the bottle with her flippers. Thunder's medallion is shining brightly in the bottle.

Both dolphins let out a sigh of relief.

"He's OK! He's OK!" Flukie jumps for joy.

"But where is he? He must be trapped somewhere!" Sapphire cries.

So the two dolphins put their heads together to think of someone who could help Thunder.

Sapphire says, "We've got to find somebody who can dive deep enough to find him."

"I've got it!" Flukie says, excited. "I know an old, giant Blue Whale who can help us. I know where he stays, when he is not out chasing after food."

Off they swim to find him. It takes them an hour to reach the place where the giant whale lives. At this moment, the old whale is hovering in the water like a gigantic blue island. Sapphire and Flukie have never seen any creature so big.

The old Blue Whale is over 100 tons and 100 feet long. It takes the dolphins a long time just to swim from his tail to his head! When they reach his head, they find that he is asleep.

His snoring is as loud as a freight train, maybe louder.

Flukie says, "Excuse me, Mr. Blue Whale." The big blue whale does not budge.

Sapphire says, "*Excuse me*, Mr. Blue Whale." Old Blue One keeps on snoring.

They both yell as loud as they can: "EXCUSE ME, MR. BLUE WHALE!!"

Slowly, slowly, Old Blue One adjusts his round, wise-looking grandpa glasses and peers out at them. He has kind old eyes.

"Yeeessssss?" he says, waking up very, very slowly. His voice booms and vibrates, even when he talks as quietly as he possibly can.

Flukie says, "It's Flukie, sir. Do you remember me?"

Old Blue says, "Oh, Flukie, yes. How could I forget you and your big tail flukes? What can I do for you today? And who is your pretty friend here?"

"This is my best friend Sapphire" Flukie says. "My other best friend Thunder is in trouble. We think you might be able to help him."

"What happened to your friend?" Old Blue One asks, with kindness in his voice.

Flukie and Sapphire explain how Thunder fell to the bottom of the ocean after he was caught in a fishing net.

"How do you know he is still alive?" Old Blue One asks, with sadness in his eyes.

Flukie and Sapphire show him the bottle. Flukie says, "This bottle popped up out of the water. His medallion was in the bottle. He is trying to tell us he is still alive!"

CHAPTER 4
Four Good Friends

Before Flukie and Sapphire visited the giant blue whale, Old Blue was feeling old and down in the dumps. He was very lonely because he had not seen his family in over two months. The younger members of his family had gone off in the vast ocean in search of massive fields of plankton* and krill* to eat.

As Old Blue One talks with Flukie and Sapphire, he feels happy for the first time since his family left. He is thinking about what he could do to help rescue Thunder.

"I'm too old to help rescue Thunder myself," he tells Flukie and Sapphire. "But I know someone who can."

"Who? Tell us!" Sapphire and Flukie yell in unison.

"Four good friends of mine," Old Blue One replies. "They are sperm whales who can dive as deep as I can, or deeper. They can also stay down under the surface for long periods of time. I know they will help you rescue your friend. Their leader's name is Corfu.* Would you like me to call him?

"Yes! Yes, oh, yes please!" say Flukie and Sapphire, swimming around each other excitedly.

"All right then, I will call him now. For your safety, please stand back while I call him. I may be a little old, but I can still send a message a long, long way! Now, get behind that huge rock over there," Old Blue One says, directing them toward the rock.

After Flukie and Sapphire are safely behind the huge rock, Old Blue One points himself in the direction he believes the sperm whales are located, and lets out a **WHALE** OF A SOUND!

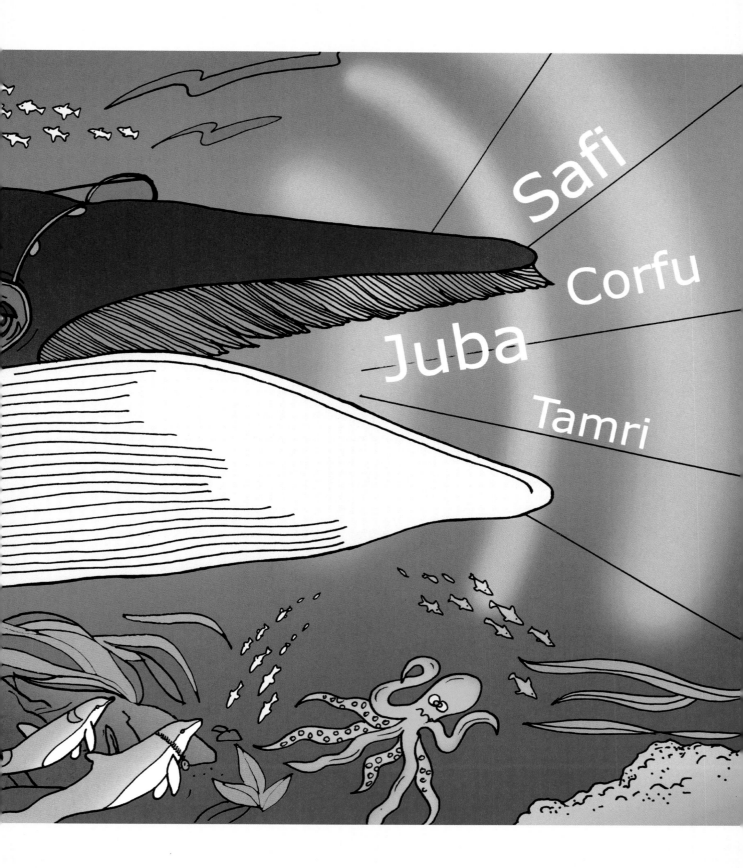

The vibrations from that blast of sound are so huge, Sapphire and Flukie shake and shudder and have to huddle behind the rock with all their might. This sound is even louder than the roar of a 747 jet airplane.

Old Blue One is calling the sperm whales by their names. The giant blue whale's cry can be heard for over 1,000 miles. The sound is echoing throughout the sea. Over and over, his message to Corfu and the other sperm whales echoes through the sea.

The sperm whales are about 800 miles south of Sapphire, Flukie, and Old Blue One. They are frolicking in the ocean off the coast Africa. The sperm whales have been hunting squid in the deepest depths of the ocean. The giant squid is the arch enemy of the sperm whale.

These whales use their clicks and sonar* to nab their prey.

One of the sperm whales receives the message from Old Blue first. His name is Safi.*

Safi alerts Corfu and the other sperm whales. They all listen in and they talk among themselves. They agree they want to help Old Blue One find Thunder.

Together, the sperm whales all let out a return call. It's another **WHALE** OF A SOUND. It says: "PLEASE TELL FLUKIE AND SAPPHIRE THEY CAN COUNT ON US! WE WILL HELP RESCUE THUNDER."

Old Blue receives the message and tells the dolphins. They are delighted! Old Blue One and the sperm whales trade a few more messages about where the sperm whales will meet Flukie and Sapphire.

"They are on their way now. They will meet you not far from here. Keep listening to their sounds and follow their location. Hurry up! Off with you now!" Old Blue Says with a flick of his tail and a sparkle in his eye.

Flukie and Sapphire speed off on their long journey to meet the four sperm whales. When they arrive and are together with the sperm whales for the first time, they become good friends right away.

"I'm Flukie. They call me that because I have big flukes," Flukie says to the four sperm whales, showing off his tail.

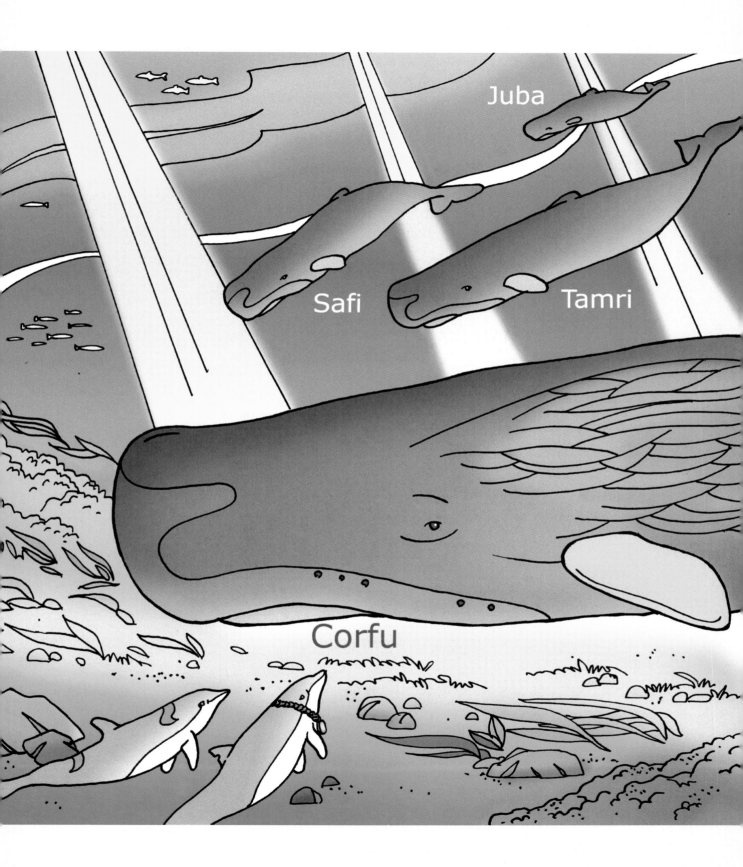

"I'm Sapphire, because I'm sparkly and blue!" says Sapphire. "We are so happy you're going to help save Thunder!"

The four sperm whales are Corfu,* Safi,* Juba,* and Tamri*. They explain to Flukie and Sapphire what their names mean.

The two dolphins tell the whales how they lost their best friend Thunder and the location where they found his medallion in the bottle.

"We know he must be OK! This is how we know," Flukie says. "See this medallion?"

The four whales peer closely at Thunder's medallion, now hanging around Flukie's neck.

"This medallion was in a bottle that popped out of the water not far from where Thunder went down," Flukie continues. "Thunder *always* wore this special medallion around his neck. He must have taken it off and put it in the bottle so we could find it, and we would know he is OK!"

"We've been in this area many times before hunting squid," Corfu says. "We know there are many underwater caves. It's likely that Thunder is in one of those caves. But they are so very deep under the water! It's very dangerous to go there."

"It's our only chance! We have to go and save Thunder!" Sapphire cries.

"Of course we will still help to rescue Thunder," Tamri says, soothing her.

"But this is going to be a long, difficult journey. We must get a good night's sleep first," says Juba.

The four whales and their new friends go off to rest. As they are logging* in the water, the dolphins curl up on the tail flukes of the big sperm whales, and they all go to sleep.

- Plankton: Tiny plants and animals that drift along with ocean currents. Whales love to eat them.

- Krill: Tiny, shrimp-type plankton that whales eat by the ton.

- Corfu: This whale was named after an island in Greece.

- Clicks and Sonar: These words describe how a whale knows about many things in the ocean. When a whale sends out a high-pitched click sound, the sound bounces off an object and some of the sound returns back to the whale. The sound returning to the whale tells the whale about the object's size, shape, distance, direction and much more.

- Safi: This whale was named after a town on the African coast in the country of Morocco.

- Juba: This whale is named after King Juba, an ancient Roman king who discovered the Canary Islands off the coast of Africa.

- Tamri: This whale is named after a town on the African coast in the country of Western Sahara.

- Logging: Logging is when a whale lies still at the surface of the water, resting, with its tail hanging down.

CHAPTER 5
The Uninvited Guest

Thunder is wondering if he will ever see his family and friends again. He swims down the long river passageway toward the dim light. The fireflies are lighting the way for him. He is following the light he saw at the far end of the passageway. The light gets brighter and brighter the nearer he swims toward it. Soon the light is all around him. He begins to hear sounds. They are beautiful sounds. Music. The music gets louder and louder.

He cannot believe what he sees before his eyes. Hundreds of sea creatures of all shapes, sizes, and colors. A lot of these strange and beautiful creatures live only deep down in the ocean, nowhere else. They are having a party in a gigantic cave room. Strange and wondrous creatures of the sea are dancing in pairs, swimming alone, and floating in groups along with the rhythm of the music.

The music comes from a band of starfish in the corner. The light shines from many of the sea creatures themselves. Lots of jellyfish and squid are giving off light from their bodies. (Please see the end of this chapter for a very long word* describing how this light can happen in the deepest, darkest depths of the ocean.)

Sparkling in the green, yellow and blue light are diamonds, emeralds, pearls, gold pieces and other gems and precious metals. The bright flashes of color and light remind Thunder for a moment of his medallion.

Fish of all kinds are drinking from golden goblets and eating off of china plates. The entire cave is filled with beautiful furniture and carved chairs that look like ancient thrones.

At one massive table, two dozen fish are noisily playing a card game. At the far end of the room a graceful sea horse is giving the children rides. A banquet table is loaded with delicious bounties of the sea. A group of shrimp in a corner of the cave are having a cocktail party. Snails are having a heated debate about the current status of Escargot.

Thunder pinches himself and wonders if he is in the midst of a dream. As he slowly swims into the room, all the creatures turn toward him in amazement.

They whisper among themselves, "What in the world is a *dolphin* doing down here?" "Where did he come from? How did he get here?"

Everyone in the room is staring at him.

Thunder feels very awkward. He stops in the middle of the room. He shrugs and says, "Well…well, um, ah……"

A big green and orange fish grabs him and says, "You need to speak to Big Sid!"

The seahorses agree and follow along, saying, "Who are you and who invited you to our party? You really need to speak to Big Sid."

Thunder yells out to the big green and orange fish, "Who is Big Sid?!"

The big green and orange fish points Thunder a little to the left, and Thunder wonders how he could have missed the sight right before his eyes. In the middle of the room, sitting high upon a royal throne on a massive stage, sits an amazing creature with many, many arms and a gigantic head.

It is a giant squid, the largest Thunder has ever seen. The giant squid turns slowly toward Thunder until they are facing each other directly. The music and dancing stops. Thunder is very scared. Then he sees the squid's face. At first the squid has a very serious look on his big face, but then he smiles as wide as the giant blue ocean. He is holding six goblets of wine in each of his arms.

His deep voice booms across the room. "Welcome to our party, Dolphin! I am Big Sid. Now, if you don't mind my asking: What is your name and how in the world did you get down here?"

24

"My name is Thunder and boy, have I got a s_
says, and tells Big Sid and all the other fish the st
They listen closely to his every word. When he ge
giant boulders covering the front of the cave and i
everyone gasps. The creatures appear to be very s_
repeating, "The boulders are covering the cave ent_
are covering the cave entrance…."

Big Sid rubs his chin and says, "You know, Mr. T_ ____ __u
be a big problem for all of us down here. Maybe you and I can help each
other out. But first, let me introduce you to all of my friends."

Big Sid slides from his massive throne down into the water. He swims
along with Thunder while introducing him to all the fish at the party.
Thunder has a wonderful time talking to all of his new friends.

Later, Thunder asks Big Sid, "Where did all this beautiful stuff
come from?"

Big Sid answers, "Most of it came from the old shipwrecks. And all
of the bright, shiny things come from a secret cave deep down inside the
Earth. We call it the Crystal Cave. The shiny things grow on all of the
walls of the cave. We make the journey to this special place several times
a year and bring back lots of shiny thing. Humans call the shiny things
diamonds, emeralds and sapphires."

Big Sid continues, "The last journey we made there, something very
scary happened. While swimming home, we were attacked by a gang of
huge, nasty creatures. You see, one of my eight arms has a big scar on it. I
had to protect all of the little creatures who were with me. We barely got
out of there with our lives."

Thunder asks, "What was it that attacked you?"

"I don't know," Big Sid replies. "It looked like a humpback whale but it
had big sharp teeth, flippers, and legs with sharp clawed feet. There was
more then one of them. They were very mean. I've been in a lot of battles
in my day. Once I found out their weakness, I caught the upper hand and
they all backed off. But these creatures meant business."

frightened just by the description of these creatures.

notices Thunder looks scared and says, "We are all OK now,
love our home. It is beautiful, isn't it?"

"It certainly is," Thunder agrees, while thinking to himself, "I must ask my Dad about these creatures and the Crystal Cave. If I could only get home."

"You are welcome to stay here with us for as long as you like," says Big Sid.

Thunder sighs. "No disrespect, sir, but I want to get back to my family and friends. Can you clear the huge rocks at the entrance of the cave so I can get out?"

"You mean so WE can get out? We need to get in and out of this cave also. We are all stuck!" says Big Sid.

"I can't help move the boulders! I can only go so deep because of the pressure of the ocean," Thunder cries.

Big Sid says kindly, "Don't worry, my little friend. First, we need to bed down for the evening, get some sleep, and we'll start early in the morning. We'll go down the river together, and when it is time for me to dive to move the boulders, you can stay at the surface where it is safe."

As Big Sid is resting that night, he is thinking about the day's events and about Thunder. He is worried. He thinks to himself, "Even if I move the boulder, I can't see any way that Thunder could get back to the surface alive.
If he can't get out of here, he might never see his family again."

- **The very long word is Bioluminescence. To pronounce this word, say it very slowly as follows: Bi-o-lu-min-ess-ence. Put the accent on the "ess" part of the word. Bioluminescence is a word that describes how some sea creatures shine brightly in the dark. They can do this because certain chemicals in their bodies produce light. Have you ever seen a firefly? Some fish have a similar ability.**

CHAPTER 6
The Hunt of the Orcas

Flukie, Sapphire, and the four sperm whales Corfu, Safi, Juba, and Tamri have begun their long journey to the underwater cave. They speed along as fast as they can until Corfu, who is in the lead, looks back at them with a warning glance.

"Listen," he says to the group as he slows down and points upward with a fin.

They all hear the dreaded humming sound above them. They are in great danger.

"That's the giant weaved catcher!" Sapphire whispers, her eyes wide with fright.

"We whales say it's the sound of the mysterious giant javelin!" says Juba.

The sperm whales know about the giant weaved catcher that traps all the creatures it can, but they are much more afraid of the mysterious giant javelin that shoots down at them so fast from above.

"The mysterious giant javelin is a sharp, fast spear that jets into the ocean," Juba explains to Sapphire and Flukie.

"It is a cruel, killing monster," Safi says.

"Yes," Tamri agrees, with tears in her eyes, "One of those things killed my uncle. The mysterious giant javelin has taken many of our family members and friends. There is nothing worse in the whole, wide ocean. When a giant javelin pierces a whale, it causes the whale to die a long and painful death."

The whales and dolphins remain as still as they possibly can. They are very, very quiet for a long time. The giant humming sound is directly above their heads.

Everyone lets out a huge sigh of relief as the humming sound passes over and fades away.

But they are not yet out of danger.

Later that day as they are cruising along, they hear wild, high-pitched shrieking sounds. The sounds get closer and closer. They swim faster, but the sound catches up with them. They are being chased. The dolphins know the scary sound all too well. It is the sound of a killer – killer whales, to be exact. These killer whales are called orcas, and they are the dreaded enemy of dolphins, whales and many other creatures who live in the sea.

Even though the orca is the biggest member of the dolphin family, they have been known to kill dolphins. The sperm whales say the orcas are the meanest killing machines in the ocean. Orcas even hunt and kill the calves* and older members of families of any creatures living in the ocean.

It's a good thing that our friends the sperm whales are about three times bigger than the orcas. The sperm whales' toothed jaws are three times stronger than the orcas' jaws.

Suddenly the orcas are swimming right alongside them. They are being hunted by the orcas. The two dolphins are protected for now because they are swimming inside the group of sperm whales, but the orcas look mean and fierce. They open their mouths wide to show off their huge, sharp teeth. Flukie and Sapphire have never been this scared in their lives, except for when Thunder got caught in the net.

In a flash, the orcas swim away from the group. "Maybe they found someone else to pick on," Tamri says, but she still sounds worried.

"No, Tamri," says Corfu. "They are trying to trick us. They'll come back. Now, everyone get ready! Prepare for battle!"

Sure enough, in a quick thrust, an orca comes charging back to the group and almost rams right into Corfu.

A fierce fight begins as Corfu dodges the orca, spins around with his tail fluke and hammers hard into the orca's side. The orca is injured and retreats a bit, but does not swim away.

Suddenly, Flukie's medallion lights up. An orca is heading straight for Sapphire! In a flash, Flukie knows he can protect Sapphire. He feels very strong and powerful. With his massive flukes, he builds up speed and rams into the orca. The orca's deadly jaws open wide, trying to catch Flukie. Our friend narrowly escapes those huge, sharp teeth.

Sapphire swims within the protected circle of the sperm whales. She knows Flukie has saved her life, and gives him a gentle stoke of her tail flipper.

Another orca swims in for an attack. Juba turns swiftly, opens his jaws of pearly white teeth, and catches the orca. Juba crunches down hard, and the orca screams in pain.

The other two orcas help their friend escape from Juba's jaws, but they don't try to fight him. They understand they are defeated. The three orcas swim away, and our friends are safe again.

"I saw Thunder's medallion flash and shine right before you protected Sapphire," Safi says to Flukie. "And there it goes again."

"Yes," Sapphire agrees. "It is shining bright with light, just like it did when Thunder found it in the ship."

Everyone in the group is very curious about the medallion as they watch it shine and flash with bright light.

"It seems to have special powers, like magic," Corfu says. "It must give some kind of special protection."

Finally, many hours after they began their long, dangerous journey, the whales and dolphins reach the place near where Thunder went down with the net.

"We must leave you here for a little while," Corfu says to Flukie and Sapphire. "It's time for us to do what we came here for – we will find the underwater cave."

"Oh, thank you, thank you for offering to rescue Thunder!" Sapphire says with tears in her eyes. "Please come back safely!"

"We will! We will!" the whales assure them, and with a sharp, strong dive straight downward, they're off.

They speed down, down, down to the deepest depths of the ocean as and most silent mysteries and wonders of the sea begin to unfold in front of their eyes.

- Another name for the orca is killer whale. Orcas are part of the dolphin family, but they eat dolphins and other ocean mammals along with fish and squid. They grow to be about 27 feet long and weigh about 8,000 - 12,000 pounds.
- Calves: Offspring (children) of sea mammals.

CHAPTER 7

The Charge of the Swordfish Patrol

On the surface, the parents of Thunder, Flukie, and Sapphire are frantic with worry. It has been many hours since they have seen their children. They have no idea what has happened. One minute all three young dolphins were swimming and racing nearby. The next minute, they were gone without a trace.

The parents had heard the dreaded humming sound. They thought their worst fears had come true. They were afraid that their children were caught in the Giant Weaved Catcher.

"We have no choice. We have to call the swordfish patrol," Thunder's dad says.

"But they are so *strange*!" says Sapphire's mom.

"Yes, they are really goofy," Flukie's mom adds. "They are always poking everybody and each other with their swords, and they tell bad jokes."

"That is true," Thunder's Dad agrees, "but they have been protecting us for many years and I think they know what they are doing."

The parents talk about what they should say and how they should contact the patrol.

"The swordfish patrol won't hear us unless many dolphins call them all at once," Sapphire's mom says. "We need at least 20 dolphins to call the patrol."

So the parents get 20 of their friends together. The whole pod wants to do whatever they can do to help Thunder, Flukie, and Sapphire.

"Listen, everyone," Thunder's dad says to the group of 20 dolphins. "At the count of three, all of us will use our clicks* and squeaks to call the swordfish patrol. Is everyone ready? One..........Two.......... THREEEEEEEE!"

All at once, an enormous rush of dolphin sounds blasts through the water. Many sea creatures hear or feel the sound. It is so loud and strong, entire schools of fish scatter around and around, confused.

Nearby, a member of the swordfish patrol hears the dolphins' sounds, loud and clear.

"That sounds like a call for help," the swordfish says. "It sounds like a very urgent call from dolphins. I'd better go get Captain Siringgo and the rest of the patrol."

Captain Siringgo and the swordfish patrol gather together as one unit. They speed quickly to where the dolphin calls are coming from. When they see the dolphins, they are still speeding fast. In fact, they run right into the dolphins. They can't halt fast enough.

There are sounds of *Boingk!* and *Bonk!* and *"Ow, Ouch!"* and *"Get that thing outta my ear!"* as Captain Siringgo and the swordfish slide into each other and the dolphins.

The captain's face is red with embarrassment.

"I see you have met my men," Captain Siringgo says to the dolphins. "I am Captain Siringgo, at your service!"

It looks like the swordfish have run into each other many times before, as their bodies are covered with little band-aids.

Captain Siringgo turns to introduce the members of his patrol, and pokes one of the other swordfish in the middle of the forehead by accident.

"Hey, watch it, Siringgo, ya blowfish!" the swordfish says. "You're as blind as a squid!"

Flukie's mom laughs. "They all look a little unruly and rough around the edges, don't they?" she whispers to Sapphire's mom.

Siringgo hears the ladies laughing and says, "We might look a little rough at the gills, but that's only because we're all in need of a good mission!"

When the men hear the Captain say the word "mission," they all perk up.

"So what can we do to help you?"

"Three of our children are missing," Thunder's dad explains. "Thunder, Flukie, and Sapphire disappeared earlier today when they were playing. We think the Giant Weaved Catcher caught them."

Captain Siringgo is scribbling notes in his official patrol sucker fish pad. (Here's another reason the captain has band-aids all over him: That sucker fish gets a tasty meal off the captain's back every day.)

"So what direction is this catcher going?" Captain Siringgo asks.

"It's heading west," Thunder's dad says.

They all look way off toward the western horizon.

The patrolmen start buzzing with excitement, saying over and over, "We have a mission. We have a mission." They all stand straight up at attention.

They see the catcher quite far off in the distance.

Captain Siringgo doesn't waste a moment.

"Men, there is our enemy. CHARGE!!!"

The swordfish cavalry trumpet is sounded, and they all speed off to battle the Giant Weaved Catcher.

The swordfish and dolphins all chase the fishing trawler. They are swimming faster than they have ever swum in their lives. Faster and faster, the pod of dolphins and swordfish speed after the boat, cutting through the water with their powerful bodies.* Finally, they catch up with the Giant Weaved Catcher. They look through the net and see hundreds of fish of all sizes and colors. Among all of those fish is a baby swordfish.

Flukie, Thunder, and Sapphire are not caught in the net. Their parents are so relieved! But at the same time, everyone feels sorry for all of those fish caught in the net. The baby swordfish is crying.

"We have to free them!" Sapphire's Mom says, and all the others agree.

But at this very moment, the Giant Weaved Catcher is being pulled up out of the water toward the deck of the fishing boat. Many fish in the net begin gasping, suddenly unable to breathe.

"We have to try to free each and every one of those creatures! We have no time to lose! To the rescue!" Captain Siringgo yells, brandishing his sword.

The swordfish surround the Giant Weaved Catcher. They cut. They thrash. They have never attempted anything like this before and they give it their best effort as they saw at the net. They cut through part of the net. Four tuna swim free. Then they cut through a quarter of the net. Out burst three fat pufferfish sisters. Finally, the net opens up all the way, and every single one of the sea creatures bursts out of the net. They jump for joy in their freedom.

All the dolphins cheer.

The swordfish patrol untangles the baby swordfish just in time, as the net is being pulled up on to the boat. The baby is so grateful to all who saved him.

"What's your name, little one?" Captain Siringgo asks.

"Blueto," the baby replies.

As the fishing boat moves on, the patrol brings Blueto over to meet everyone who had helped to save him - the swordfish patrol and the dolphins and all the fish.

"May I have your attention please," Captain Siringgo says to the group. "I would now like to introduce our new friend Blueto, the youngest member of the swordfish patrol!"

Everyone claps and cheers as they celebrate this miracle. None of the dolphins had ever seen any creature saved from the weaved catcher before.

But they are still very worried and scared. Thunder, Flukie, and Sapphire have been gone for too long.

The dolphins talk to the swordfish with newfound respect. Together, the group decides that they would have better luck finding the three dolphins if they split up. The patrolmen say they will keep looking in this area.

As night falls and a blazing red-orange sunset sinks over the western horizon, they thank each other and go their separate ways.

• **One dolphin has the power of two men.**

CHAPTER 8

Juba and the Rescue

Flukie and Sapphire are swimming back up to the surface, talking about how grateful they are to the sperm whales for protecting them from the Orcas. As they are moving on, they see an amazing sight. Five humpback whales and a calf are playing. Even though Flukie and Sapphire are upset about their friend Thunder, they love to watch the whales dip and spin. The humpbacks whales have longer flippers than any other kind of whale. When they play with their calves* underwater, it's like watching a ballet.

Flukie and Sapphire are in a trance of delight by the dance of the humpback whales. They watch for as long as they can, then move on.

Soon they meet up with Old Blue One at the surface.

"Ah, there you are, my little friends," says the Old Blue One, with a big smile stretching across his gigantic, kind face. "Did you find the four sperm whales who said they would help Thunder?"

Excited to tell their story, Sapphire says, "Yes, we did! They saved our lives! They protected us from Orcas who were trying to attack us. And now, Corfu, Safi, Juba, and Tamri are going to the underwater cave to rescue Thunder."

"That is good news," Old Blue One says.

Corfu, Safi, Juba, and Tamri are still traveling far downward to find the cave where Thunder is trapped. On the way, they see many underwater caves. They stop at each cave entrance and peer inside. They find one cave that is totally blocked by huge boulders.

"What's that?" says Tamri to the others, pointing to something twisted on a nearby rock.

"Why, that is a ragged, twisted piece of fishing net!" Corfu says. "I think this must be the cave where Thunder is trapped."

"Well, how are we going to get him out of there? Those boulders must weigh a ton or more!" Safi says.

"Let's ram them!" Juba says. "I know we can do it!"

It's very possible the whales could do it. Each sperm whale weighs about 40 tons and is 50 feet long. They are quite powerful creatures.

Safi goes first. He rears back, races towards the boulders and rams them hard! The boulders barely budge, but they do move a tiny bit.

Next up is Tamri. She's also very strong. She races in from the other direction and crashes into the boulders with a huge thud. Two boulders fall out of the way.

Corfu comes rushing in and hits another huge boulder out of the way, and finally, Juba knocks out the last and biggest of the boulders.

But this creates a huge avalanche. Boulders tumble down and close up the entrance of the cave once more. The huge rocks also fall right on top of Juba.

"Oh no! Juba! Are you OK?" Corfu yells after the avalanche has stopped shaking and rocking everything.

"I don't know," Juba says. "I can't move much."

The 40-ton whale is now trapped at 1,800 feet below the surface of the water.

Corfu, Tamri, and Safi try to move the boulders off Juba. Again and again they push the rocks and ram them just as they did before, but no luck.

They are running out of time to rescue Juba before he runs out of air. His life is in danger now with every minute that goes by.

- **Calves: Baby whales**
- **The Humpback whales' flippers are about the same size as the Blue whales' flippers.**

CHAPTER 9
Tonga the Great Blue Whale

At daybreak, Thunder and Big Sid decide to swim down the river passageway toward the cave entrance. Big Sid stops Thunder and says, "You stay here. I'm going to dive down and try to move the boulders." Big Sid disappears down through the passageway.

As Big Sid gets to the boulder wall, he hears roaring and rumbling outside the cave. He also hears the cries of whales. The rumblings and whale sounds are very loud at first, then become quiet. This is the same underwater avalanche that traps Juba right outside the cave.

Big Sid presses his giant body and long tentacles with their suction cups against the boulders. He can't move them. He tries again, but with no luck. He says to himself, "I just cannot move these boulders. I know Thunder will be very disappointed."

He swims up through the passageway to the surface of the underwater river cave, where he sees Thunder.

"We are still trapped, my friend," Big Sid tells Thunder sadly.

They are both disappointed and scared.

Back at the surface, Flukie, Sapphire, and Old Blue One are talking about what they can do to help the sperm whales rescue Thunder. Suddenly they hear shrieking across the ocean. A giant wave is coming at them with a rush and a roar. As it gets closer and closer, the shrieks become louder and clearer.

Old Blue One says with a big smile on his face, "I believe it is my family. They have finally come home from the feeding grounds!"

Five mammoth blue whales approach slowly.

"I have missed you so much!" Old Blue One says to his family. They are all very happy to see each other after several months apart.

"These are my friends Flukie and Sapphire," Old Blue says. "Their friend Thunder is trapped in an underwater cave far, far down below. Four sperm whales went down there to help rescue him. I have not heard from them in awhile. I hope they are all right."

"We'll go find out, Dad!" says Old Blue One's biggest son, Tonga. "Stand back, Flukie and Sapphire! We are going down."

The five massive blue whales dive down deep. As they near the underwater caves, they meet with Corfu, leader of the sperm whales.

"Thunder is still in the cave," Corfu explains. "There was an avalanche and now our friend Juba is trapped too! We couldn't move the boulders. Juba will run out of air if we don't help him."

"No problem," all the huge blue whales say in unison. "Let's go get Juba and Thunder out of there!"

The whales swim to the underwater cave and plan their strategy.

Tonga finds the place where Juba is trapped under the gigantic boulders. Then he does something quite amazing. He picks up the boulder in his mouth, and tosses it out of the way. The sperm whales admire the massive blue whale's incredible strength.

Tonga's brother, as if he is a mammoth bulldozer, pushes the other boulders off Juba with his nose. Juba is now free.

"Are you OK, Juba?" Tonga asks, as they swim back to the other whales.

Juba answers, "I'm a little sore, but I'll be fine."

Before they can go back to help Thunder, all of the whales head up to the surface for a dose of fresh air.

Now imagine this: Here are five 100-ton blue whales and four 44-ton sperm whales – nine whales altogether. As the thundering whales come rushing to the top, the whales blast through the surface of the water with a tremendous roar! It is almost overwhelming for Flukie and Sapphire and Old Blue to see.

The whales tell Old Blue, Flukie, and Sapphire that Juba is OK and that they are going to get some air and go back down to find Thunder. The whales all go back down together to clear the rest of the boulders from the blocked cave entrance.

The blue whales remove all the boulders. When the cave is clear, the blue whales see that their job is finished. They are so large that they can't fit into the cave entrance.

The sperm whales can fit, though. "I'll go in there and search for Thunder," Corfu volunteers.

"OK. We'll stay here and will be ready to help if you need us," Tonga says.

Corfu heads into the cave and goes upwards and into the passageway. He reaches the surface of the underwater river and pops up into the river cave. He takes a fresh breath of air and looks around.

"Thunder must be here somewhere," he says to himself. In fact, Thunder and Big Sid are swimming in this same river, back to the community of creatures in the cave.

Corfu sees a dim light at the end of the cave, the same light Thunder had seen when he first got to this river. He thinks he sees something swimming far up ahead. He puts out a call for Thunder and eagerly waits for an answer.

Thunder and Big Sid hear the call and stop in amazement. Thunder replies, "I am here. I am here!"

Thunder and Big Sid swim quickly toward the direction of Corfu's call. Thunder swims ahead and is surprised to meet up with a giant sperm whale. Corfu says, "Are you Mr. Thunder?"

"Why, yes! I am Thunder, and I've never been so happy to see a sperm whale! Where did you come from?"

"I'll tell you the whole story later. Blue whales and sperm whales have had many adventures trying to rescue you. Your friends Flukie and Sapphire got the rescue effort going."

Thunder says, "I've met an incredible group of sea creatures down here, and my friend right behind me......"

Suddenly, Corfu's eyes get big and he arches his back, as if to either attack something or protect himself.

Big Sid the squid, and all 30 feet of his massive body, comes up behind Thunder. Big Sid sees Corfu and immediately backs off. His eyes are terrified.

Sperm whales and squid are arch enemies. Whenever they come into contact, one of them usually is killed or hurt.

Thunder understands what is happening.

"Now you two, settle down! *Please* settle down," Thunder says. "We can all act like gentlemen. There is no need to fight."

Thunder turns to Big Sid and says, "This sperm whale risked his life trying to clear the cave entrance for us!"

Big Sid sighs. "I guess you are right, Thunder." He turns to Corfu and says, "You have nothing to fear from me, Mr. Sperm Whale. Plus, Thunder is a friend to both of us. We have Thunder's rescue in common, and we both want him safely returned to his family and friends. Let's put our differences aside for today."

Corfu grumbles but agrees, "Yes, if only for today."

Thunder says, "Big Sid, thank you for all of your help! You are truly a friend of mine for life. I will never forget your kindness for as long as I live. Please tell all of the creatures back at the cave that they have my sincere thanks and gratitude."

They shake flippers and tentacles and give each other a huge hug. Big Sid swims back down the river to tell all the fish that they are no longer trapped in the cave.

Thunder and Corfu head back the other way, toward the cave entrance. "Thank you! Thank you for saving my life, Corfu! But….I hate to ask this, but…. how can I get out of here? I was inside a protective bubble when I entered the cave. My body can't survive the pressure of the ocean depths. I'm afraid I will not make it."

Corfu is very interested in what Thunder is saying. "I was wondering how you got down here," Corfu says. "Please tell me all about this protective bubble."

"It is a long story. I'll tell you about it some other time," Thunder responds.

Corfu wonders how in the world he is going to get Thunder out of the cave alive. Suddenly he gets an idea.

"I know exactly how we can do this," Corfu says. "Stay here, Thunder. I'll be right back." Corfu swims down the passageway. Deeper and deeper down he goes, until he gets to the cave entrance where his friends are waiting.

CHAPTER 10

Tonga the Pressure Chamber

Corfu, Juba, Safi, Tamri and all five of the massive blue whales swim back up to the surface of the ocean for a quick breath of fresh air.

Corfu tells them, "I have rescued Thunder, but he is still in danger in the underwater river. This river is above the cave entrance. You have to swim up a long underwater passageway to get to the river inside the tunnel. The pressure is normal where I left him, but if he has to dive into the passageway toward the entrance of the cave, the pressure is too much. The pressure would also be dangerous for him on the way back up to the surface of the ocean. He would not survive the whole journey. So I thought up an idea of how the blue whales can help out. Would you like to hear this idea?"

"Yes, of course!" Tonga says. "We will help out any way we can. What is your idea, Corfu?"

"I was thinking that I would enter the cave and get Thunder. Then, Thunder and I would swim down the passageway. When we get to the cave entrance, I would ask Tonga to open his massive mouth around the entrance. Tonga, you could seal off the cave entrance with your mouth! Thunder would swim right into your gigantic mouth. As big as you are, the pressure would be balanced inside your mouth. That means Thunder could get all the way back up to the surface of the ocean safely."

Tonga says, "I am the one for this job! Let's go."

All the whales take a deep breath and dive back down to the cave entrance. Corfu enters the cave first. Just past the cave entrance, Corfu looks back and sees the gigantic blue whale Tonga's nose.

Corfu swims up the cave passageway toward the river and Thunder. He pops up at the surface of the river where Thunder waits patiently.

"You're going to get out of here, Thunder! A massive blue whale will put his mouth into the entrance to the cave. We will swim back down to the entrance and when we see the blue whale Tonga, I'll ask him to open his mouth and you will swim in. Then he will close his giant mouth and slowly take you to the surface of the ocean. Do you think you can make it to the cave entrance?"

Thunder thinks for a minute and says, "I've done it once before, but the pressure of the ocean was very painful."

Corfu says, "All we can do is try. You can't stay here. So let's go!"

Corfu keeps his eye on Thunder as they swim together down through the passageway to the cave entrance. Deeper and deeper they go. At first Thunder's body aches, but he can take it. But soon, every bone and muscle is blazing with pain. Corfu notices the look of extreme pain on Thunder's face. Thunder slows down, barely able to move. Corfu stops Thunder and asks him if he is OK.

"I think I can make it," Thunder says.

"Hang in there, Thunder. Keep going! Don't stop now! We are almost there!"

But Thunder is about to faint with pain and weakness. The world around him is beginning to grow darker and darker. His eyes close.

At that moment, Corfu grabs Thunder's flipper.

"We've made it to the entrance! Come on!"

Thunder can barely hear him. He starts to drift away…

"Tonga! Open your mouth! We're here!" Corfu yells.

Tonga places his mouth onto the entrance of the cave. His mouth is so massive, it seals off the entrance to the cave. Corfu guides Thunder gently onto the whale's tongue, which is the size of a car.

Tonga closes his mouth very gently, and very slowly backs away from the cave. Thunder is now inside an airtight chamber that protects him from the pressure of the ocean depths.

Tonga, Corfu, and the other whales travel back up to the surface of the ocean very slowly. This helps to even out the pressure on Thunder's body. 1,800 feet, 1,500 feet, 1,000 feet, 600 feet, 300 feet and up to the surface they float.

All the whales come to the surface of the water slowly where Flukie, Sapphire, and Old Blue are waiting.

"Where is Thunder? Where is Thunder? Is he OK???" the dolphins ask.

"We're about to find out! Watch my big brother Tonga!" one of the whales says.

Tonga opens his mouth slowly. Thunder lays motionless on the blue whale's huge tongue. Flukie and Sapphire swim over to look into Tonga's mouth. Thunder doesn't move.

"Thunder, please wake up. Please wake up!! Thunder, we need you!" Thunder does not respond.

"Please Thunder. Please WAKE UP!!!" Flukie screams.

Thunder's flippers slowly move. His body moves just a little. He opens his eyes just a crack. In a soft and muffled voice, he asks, "Is that you, Flukie? Is that you, Sapphire? Can it be true???"

Flukie and Sapphire cry out in joy. "Thunder! Thunder, you're OK!"

They help Thunder out of the giant blue whale's mouth, pat him on the shoulders with their flippers, and tell him to take it easy as they hover around him like protective pals.

"I think we have something that belongs to you, Thunder," Flukie says. As he places the medallion around Thunder's neck, the medallion glows and flashes brightly for a moment. All the whales see the medallion flash and are amazed.

CHAPTER 11
Back Home Safe and Sound

The blue whales and sperm whales float in a circle around Old Blue, who is so proud of all they have done.

Old Blue says to the group, "Today, friends and enemies alike, old and young, have come together like we always have, to rescue a dear friend. We have put aside our differences to bring Thunder back to his family and friends."

Thunder, Flukie, and Sapphire are there, too. They swim around the circle of whales, thanking each one with hugs and flipper-shakes. They swim to the center of the circle and give a special goodbye and hug to Old Blue One.

"If it weren't for you, we would never have seen Thunder again," Sapphire says to Old Blue, with a tear in her eye.

"I don't know how I can ever repay you and the whales for rescuing me," Thunder tells him.

"Your loyal friendship and gratitude are the best reward you can ever give us," the wise old whale tells the three young dolphins. "Now, off you go. Your parents have missed you!"

On their way home, Thunder, Flukie, and Sapphire run into the swordfish patrol.

"Well, there you are! All safe and sound, I see!" Captain Siringgo says to the three young dolphins.

"Yes, sir. We're on our way home now," Thunder says.

"Your parents have been very worried about you. I'll have a special patrol swim ahead and tell them you're on your way."

Suddenly a swordfish named Rudor swims by very fast. He has a big fishing hook in his mouth, and the hook is pulling a fishing pole. A chubby little man is holding on to the fishing pole. The man is saying something nobody understands. To them, it just sounds like "Blub Blub BLUB!"

In human talk, that means, "Hey, you crazy fish! Where are you taking me? I'm supposed to catch YOU. Not the other way around!"

But whenever a man talks, all the fish can understand is "Blub Blub BLUB!"

The fish translate the word "man" as "knucklehead" in their language.

The knucklehead is being pulled very fast through the water.

Rudor is calling to Captain Sirginggo:

"Boss! Boss! I caught one! I caught a knucklehead!"

Rudor circles the swordfish and dolphins.

"What do I do with him, boss?"

Captain Sirginggo says, "Throw him back! What would we do with a knucklehead down here?"

Rudor spits out the hook, saying, "I can't have any fun anymore around here!"

The knucklehead swims back up to the surface, saying "Blub, blub BLEEP!"

Thunder, Flukie and Sapphire wave goodbye as the patrol swims off.

Soon, they see their mothers, fathers, sisters, brothers, aunts, uncles, and cousins – the whole pod is there to welcome them back home.

Thunder's mother and father have tears in their eyes as they hug their son.

"At first we were very angry with you for being gone so long. Then we were scared, and then we were frantic!" Thunder's mom says.

"Tell us what happened!" says Thunder's dad.

Sapphire begins to describe their adventure, starting with Thunder being caught in the piece of fishing net and falling down, down, down into the farthest depths of the ocean.

"You could have drowned! What saved you?" Thunder's mom cries.

Thunder explains, "My medallion kept illuminating, and there was this magic bubble that saved my life."

Thunder's dad says, "Did you say the medallion illuminated? You know what history has said about the old medallion, don't you? For centuries the tale of the magic medallion has been told, but I had no idea it could be the one you have worn around your neck."

Thunder's father explains the old legend further: "If your intentions are good, the medallion will protect you and guide you safely to your home. If your intentions are bad, the medallion will work against you."

Flukie's mom asks, "Where did you say you found this medallion?"

"In an old sunken pirate ship!" Flukie answers. "I bet there are more treasures down there. Want to go see?"

"Yes!" All the dolphins say in unison, because even grown-up dolphins love to explore and play.

Thunder says, "On the count of three, let's dive down! I'll show you how to get there. One, Two, Three!!!"

All the dolphins dive down together to explore the sunken treasures. Who knows what they might find next? One thing you know for certain: our friends the dolphins and thundering whales will have many more adventures together, in the ocean off the coast of the Emerald Isle.

About the Author

Stephen Vadakin is an artist and author known for his museum-quality sculptures of marine mammals. He also created an educational program about marine life that he has brought to more than 50,000 elementary school children. He began his work as an artist after a deeply inspirational experience he had while sailing. He had lost his way, and while he was on his radio seeking help, twelve dolphins approached his sailboat. They bumped the boat and jumped out of the water while talking to Stephen with their clicks and squeaks, staying with him until he found his way back. His research into how dolphins and whales communicate led him to write *"The Adventures of the Thundering Whales."*

Acknowledgments

This book would not have happened without the love of my parents,
who have been there for me every step of the way. I would also like
to thank my editor Julie Wichman and all of the children who will
read this book.

59950869R00035